Hello, Family Members,

Learning to read is one of the most important accomplishments of early childhood. **Hello Reader!** books are designed to help children become skilled readers who like to read. Beginning readers learn to read by remembering frequently used words like "the," "is," and "and"; by using phonics skills to decode new words; and by interpreting picture and text clues. These books provide both the stories children enjoy and the structure they need to read fluently and independently. Here are suggestions for helping your child *before*, *during*, and *after* reading:

Before

- Look at the cover and pictures and have your child predict what the story is about.
- Read the story to your child.
- Encourage your child to chime in with familiar words and phrases.
- Echo read with your child by reading a line first and having your child read it after you do.

During

- Have your child think about a word he or she does not recognize right away. Provide hints such as "Let's see if we know the sounds" and "Have we read other words like this one?"
- Encourage your child to use phonics skills to sound out new words.
- Provide the word for your child when more assistance is needed so that he or she does not struggle and the experience of reading with you is a positive one.
- Encourage your child to have fun by reading with a lot of expression . . . like an actor!

After

- Have your child keep lists of interesting and favorite words.
- Encourage your child to read the books over and over again. Have him or her read to brothers, sisters, grandparents, and even teddy bears. Repeated readings develop confidence in young readers.
- Talk about the stories. Ask and answer questions. Share ideas about the funniest and most interesting characters and events in the stories.

I do hope that you and your child enjoy this book.

— Francie Alexander
Chief Education Officer,
Scholastic's Learning Ventures

D0181529

To Justin
— M.P.

To Chris Dahlen
— T.W.

Go to scholastic.com for web site information on
Scholastic authors and illustrators.

No part of this publication may be reproduced, or stored in a retrieval system, or transmitted
in any form or by any means, electronic, mechanical, photocopying, recording, or otherwise,
without written permission of the publisher. For information regarding permission, write to
Scholastic Inc., Attention: Permissions Department, 555 Broadway, New York, NY 10012.

ISBN: 0-439-32102-6

Copyright © 2001 by Nancy Hall, Inc.
All rights reserved. Published by Scholastic Inc.
SCHOLASTIC, HELLO READER, CARTWHEEL BOOKS, and associated logos
are trademarks and/or registered trademarks of Scholastic Inc.

Library of Congress Cataloging-in-Publication Data is available.

10 9 8 7 6 5 4 3 2   01 02 03 04 05
Printed in the U.S.A.
First printing, December 2001

The Christmas Penguin

by Mary Packard
Illustrated by Teri Weidner

Hello Reader! — Level 1

SCHOLASTIC INC.

New York   Toronto   London   Auckland   Sydney
Mexico City   New Delhi   Hong Kong

"Dear Santa," wrote Rollie,
"I know penguins don't fly.
But I sure wish that I
could give it a try.

For Christmas I don't want
a train or a bear.
But I'd like to be able
to fly through the air."

Rollie finished his letter
and mailed it that day.
He called all his friends
and went off to play.

They slid down big hills
that were covered with snow,
then landed—*kerplunk*—
in the water below.

Rollie's wings were like fins—
he could swim anywhere.
But try as he might,
they would not work in air.

Then late Christmas Eve,
Rollie slept in his bed.
But a flashing light turned
his bedroom bright red.

A voice woke him up.
"Rise and shine!" it cried.
Rollie rubbed his eyes
and saw Santa outside!

Rollie climbed through the window
into Santa's big sleigh.
Before Rollie knew it,
they were both on their way.

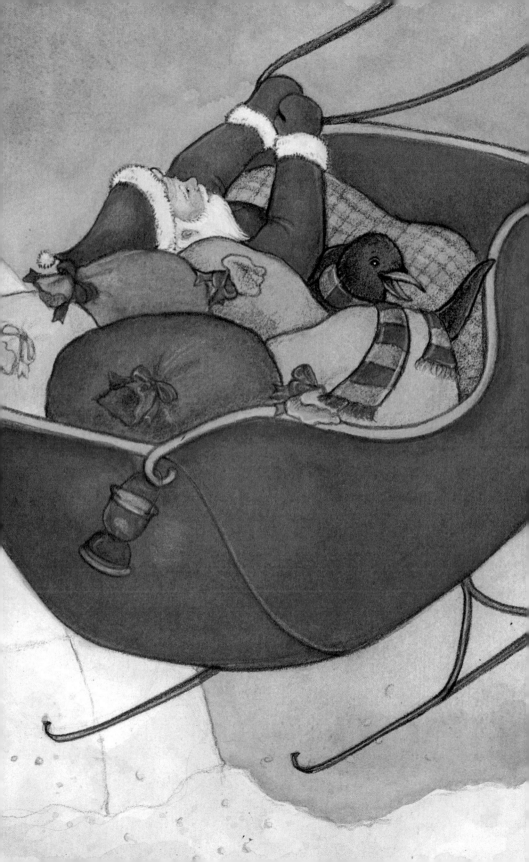

A strong polar wind
pushed the sleigh very fast.
Rollie's wish had come true:
He was flying at last!

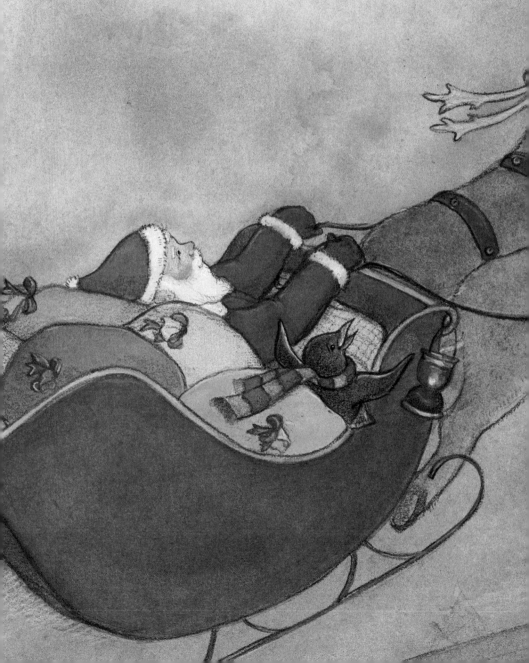

The blustery wind
blew them every which way,
and a sack full of toys
fell right off the sleigh.

Santa tried to catch it—
but he was too slow.
They watched the sack fall
to the water below.

Santa landed the sleigh
and reached for the sack.
But it sank in the water.
He could not get it back.

"I'll find it!" cried Rollie.
He dived in with a splash.
He swam to the bottom
and was back in a flash.

"Amazing!" said Santa. "There's nobody who could fly through the water faster than you!"

"It's true!" Rollie cried.
"I guess you could say
we penguins *do* fly—
in our own special way."

Then Rollie helped Santa
deliver the toys
all over the world
to good girls and boys.

"Thank you," called Santa.
"You're my special elf.
So always remember:
Be proud of yourself!"